Ca

D1576583

CR

This book m   three weeks. It is
returned on /   e last date stamp
fine of 25c w   arged for every
   eek a book is overdue.

Gelert the Brave

First published in 2008 by
Franklin Watts
338 Euston Road
London
NW1 3BH

Franklin Watts Australia
Level 17/207 Kent Street
Sydney
NSW 2000

A CIP catalogue record for this book is available
from the British Library.

ISBN 978 0 7496 7999 6 (hbk)
ISBN 978 0 7496 8007 7 (pbk)

Series Editor: Melanie Palmer
Series Advisor: Dr Barrie Wade
Series Designer: Peter Scoulding

Printed in China

Franklin Watts is a division of
Hachette Children's Books,
an Hachette Livre UK company
www.hachettelivre.co.uk

HOPSCOTCH MYTHS

Gelert the Brave

by Barrie Wade and Peter Utton

W
FRANKLIN WATTS
LONDON•SYDNEY

Once there was a lord who
lived in a castle on a hill.
He loved to go hunting.

The lord had many hunting dogs
but Gelert was his favourite.
He always took Gelert with
him as he was the best hunter.

The lord and Gelert spent many days hunting together in the forest. They always had lots of fun.

One morning, the lord got ready to
go hunting. Gelert ran to his side.

"No, Gelert, not you," said the lord.

"Stay here and guard my son,"
he ordered. So Gelert lay down
by the baby's cot.

It was quiet in the castle when the lord left, but Gelert sensed danger. Then a huge wolf appeared and crept right up to the baby's cot.

As the wolf came closer to the cot,
Gelert jumped at its throat.

The wolf twisted away. It dug
its teeth deep into Gelert's side.

Gelert scratched at the wolf's face and bit one of its paws. Angrily the wolf flung Gelert into the cot, knocking it over. The baby fell out.

As the wolf tried to reach the
baby, Gelert bit deep into its
throat. The wolf limped away.

Gelert crawled back to the broken
cot and lay next to the sleeping
baby. There was blood everywhere.

Then the lord came back. "Here, Gelert! Here, boy!" he called.

Gelert heard his master shouting
but he was too weak to respond.

The lord marched into the hall
and saw the dreadful mess.
The cot was knocked over and
his baby son was missing.

Gelert heard his master shouting but he was too weak to respond.

The lord marched into the hall and saw the dreadful mess. The cot was knocked over and his baby son was missing.

Then he saw Gelert with blood
around his mouth!

The lord raised his sword in fury and thrust it deep into Gelert's body. The dog sank down dead.

Suddenly, the lord heard a tiny cry.
He looked behind the cot and saw
his baby son.

26

Then his men entered the hall.
They pointed to a wolf's body
under the table.

At once everything was clear.
Gelert had not killed the child.
Instead the brave dog had
guarded the child with his life.

The lord wept for Gelert and
promised to honour him.

The lord built a special grave for Gelert. Everyone in the land came to honour the faithful hunting dog.

People can still visit Gelert's grave today and read all about Gelert the Brave.

Hopscotch has been specially designed to fit the requirements of the National Literacy Strategy. It offers real books by top authors and illustrators for children developing their reading skills. There are 63 Hopscotch stories to choose from:

Marvin, the Blue Pig
ISBN 978 0 7496 4619 6

Plip and Plop
ISBN 978 0 7496 4620 2

The Queen's Dragon
ISBN 978 0 7496 4618 9

Flora McQuack
ISBN 978 0 7496 4621 9

Willie the Whale
ISBN 978 0 7496 4623 3

Naughty Nancy
ISBN 978 0 7496 4622 6

Run!
ISBN 978 0 7496 4705 6

The Playground Snake
ISBN 978 0 7496 4706 3

"Sausages!"
ISBN 978 0 7496 4707 0

Bear in Town
ISBN 978 0 7496 5875 5

Pippin's Big Jump
ISBN 978 0 7496 4710 0

Whose Birthday Is It?
ISBN 978 0 7496 4709 4

**The Princess and
the Frog**
ISBN 978 0 7496 5129 9

Flynn Flies High
ISBN 978 0 7496 5130 5

Clever Cat
ISBN 978 0 7496 5131 2

Moo!
ISBN 978 0 7496 5332 3

Izzie's Idea
ISBN 978 0 7496 5334 7

Roly-poly Rice Ball
ISBN 978 0 7496 5333 0

I Can't Stand It!
ISBN 978 0 7496 5765 9

Cockerel's Big Egg
ISBN 978 0 7496 5767 3

How to Teach a Dragon Manners
ISBN 978 0 7496 5873 1

**The Truth about those
Billy Goats**
ISBN 978 0 7496 5766 6

**Marlowe's Mum and
the Tree House**
ISBN 978 0 7496 5874 8

**The Truth about
Hansel and Gretel**
ISBN 978 0 7496 4708 7

The Best Den Ever
ISBN 978 0 7496 5876 2

ADVENTURES

Aladdin and the Lamp
ISBN 978 0 7496 6692 7

Blackbeard the Pirate
ISBN 978 0 7496 6690 3

George and the Dragon
ISBN 978 0 7496 6691 0

Jack the Giant-Killer
ISBN 978 0 7496 6693 4

TALES OF KING ARTHUR

1. The Sword in the Stone
ISBN 978 0 7496 6694 1

2. Arthur the King
ISBN 978 0 7496 6695 8

3. The Round Table
ISBN 978 0 7496 6697 2

**4. Sir Lancelot and
the Ice Castle**
ISBN 978 0 7496 6698 9

TALES OF ROBIN HOOD

Robin and the Knight
ISBN 978 0 7496 6699 6

Robin and the Monk
ISBN 978 0 7496 6700 9

Robin and the Silver Arrow
ISBN 978 0 7496 6703 0

Robin and the Friar
ISBN 978 0 7496 6702 3

FAIRY TALES

The Emperor's New Clothes
ISBN 978 0 7496 7421 2

Cinderella
ISBN 978 0 7496 7417 5

Snow White
ISBN 978 0 7496 7418 2

Jack and the Beanstalk
ISBN 978 0 7496 7422 9

The Three Billy Goats Gruff
ISBN 978 0 7496 7420 5

The Pied Piper of Hamelin
ISBN 978 0 7496 7419 9

**Goldilocks and the
Three Bears**
ISBN 978 0 7496 7903 3

Hansel and Gretel
ISBN 978 0 7496 7904 0

The Three Little Pigs
ISBN 978 0 7496 7905 7

Rapunzel
ISBN 978 0 7496 7906 4

Little Red Riding Hood
ISBN 978 0 7496 7907 1

Rumpelstiltskin
ISBN 978 0 7496 7908 8

HISTORIES

**Toby and the Great Fire of
London**
ISBN 978 0 7496 7410 6

Pocahontas the Peacemaker
ISBN 978 0 7496 7411 3

Grandma's Seaside Bloomers
ISBN 978 0 7496 7412 0

Hoorah for Mary Seacole
ISBN 978 0 7496 7413 7

**Remember the 5th
of November**
ISBN 978 0 7496 7414 4

**Tutankhamun and the Golden
Chariot**
ISBN 978 0 7496 7415 1

MYTHS

Icarus, the Boy Who Flew
ISBN 978 0 7496 7992 7 *
ISBN 978 0 7496 8000 8

**Perseus and the
Snake Monster**
ISBN 978 0 7496 7993 4 *
ISBN 978 0 7496 8001 5

**Odysseus and the
Wooden Horse**
ISBN 978 0 7496 7994 1 *
ISBN 978 0 7496 8002 2

**Persephone and the
Pomegranate Seeds**
ISBN 978 0 7496 7995 8 *
ISBN 978 0 7496 8003 9

Romulus and Remus
ISBN 978 0 7496 7996 5 *
ISBN 978 0 7496 8004 6

Thor's Hammer
ISBN 978 0 7496 7997 2*
ISBN 978 0 7496 8005 3

No Dinner for Anansi
ISBN 978 0 7496 7998 9 *
ISBN 978 0 7496 8006 0

Gelert the Brave
ISBN 978 0 7496 7999 6*
ISBN 978 0 7496 8007 7

* hardback

People can still visit Gelert's grave
today and read all about Gelert
the Brave.

Hopscotch has been specially designed to fit the requirements of the National Literacy Strategy. It offers real books by top authors and illustrators for children developing their reading skills. There are 63 Hopscotch stories to choose from:

* hardback